The Lost Kitten

For Lottie and Grandma

J.S

ORCHARD BOOKS
338 Euston Road, London NW1 3BH
Orchard Books Australia
Level 17/207 Kent Street, Sydney, NSW 2000

First published in 2010 by Orchard Books

A Paperback Original

ISBN 978 1 40831 136 3

Text © Justine Smith 2010
Illustrations © Orchard Books 2010

A CIP catalogue record for this book is available
from the British Library.

1 3 5 7 9 10 8 6 4 2

Printed in the UK

Orchard Books is a division of Hachette Children's Books,
an Hachette UK company.

www.hachette.co.uk

The Lost Kitten

Justine Smith

ORCHARD BOOKS

Chapter One

The first time she saw the kittens, Alice was with Grandma. She might have known it was going to be a special day, because more often than not, when Grandma came over to look after her, something unexpected happened...

Alice lived on one side of a big park, and Grandma on the other. Alice could see the main park gates and the bus stop

from her bedroom window. Most days after
school and often during the holidays,
Grandma got on the bus at her house and
opened her book, and exactly two chapters
later, got off at the stop outside Alice's flat.
She always came with delicious snacks, and
an interesting plan.

When Alice heard the bus, she flung open
her window, leaned out and waved at
Grandma.

"What are we doing today?" she called
down.

"Let's go exploring!" said Grandma.

"Wait there, I'm coming down!"

They went across the road and in
through the park gates.

It was Alice who saw it first – a rusty gate
in the old wall, half-hidden in tangled ivy.
They had to lift the heavy creepers to
push it open. They stepped into a jungle
of overgrown bushes.

It was the end of
the summer –
the flowers
had finished
blooming,
and there was
a carpet of
old rose petals
scattered on
the ground.
The air was
sweetly perfumed.

"Goodness," said Grandma. "It's an
old rose garden!"

Tangled weeds choked the ancient, knotty bushes. Tufts of lavender struggled up towards the light. The grass almost came up to Alice's waist. An old bench leaned against crumbling red brick.

"Look, it was once a walled garden," said Grandma.

"It looks as though no one has been here for a long time," whispered Alice. "It's a secret garden!"

A flash of grey caught Alice's eye. Over by the wall, a little cat was crouched underneath the twisty rose bushes. She was studying them, her yellow eyes unblinking.

"She's so beautiful..." said Alice, with a pang. She had wanted a cat her whole life, but they weren't allowed pets in the flat.

"Hello, girl," she called to the cat. "Come and say hello?" But the cat turned around and disappeared into the ivy.

"I don't think she's tame," said Grandma. "I think this is Gypsy, the park cat. She never goes hungry, because she belongs to everyone who lives on the roads around the park."

They poked around in the overgrown flower beds. Grandma was moving the weeds aside with her stick and finding little treasures, like a row of tiny wild strawberry plants under the roses, and saying things like, "Old-fashioned tea roses – I haven't seen those since I was a girl!" and, "Look at that! A rare china

9

rose!" and, "Well, this IS a treat!" Alice was thinking that technically, since she lived so close to the park, this little cat must partly belong to her too, which was almost like having a cat of her own, but not quite...

Then Alice heard something.

"Yes, I can hear it, too," said Grandma. It was a faint *meeiou-meeiou* sound.

"I think it's coming from the ivy," said Alice. She had an inkling of what it might be, and *bang-bang*, her heart hammered at the thought that she might possibly be right.

They peered into the gloom, Alice leaning so far in that she almost fell head-first into the prickly bushes, and Grandma had to hang onto her arm. They could hear the baby-*meeiou!* sound

more clearly now, and they could just
make out the shape of the mother cat,
standing guard.

"Oh! It is! It *has* to be kittens!" said Alice, in a thrilled, squeaky voice. And she leaned even further in, trying to catch a glimpse of them. But the mother cat shrank back, and gave a low growl.

"We need to leave them in peace," said Grandma, backing out of the bush, and tugging Alice out with her. "I should think they're newborn, and we really don't want to upset the mother."

An idea popped into Alice's head. She clutched Grandma's hand. "Are these homeless kittens, do you think Grandma?" she said.

Grandma looked down at her. "Hmm," she said. "What are you plotting, Alice Allen? Didn't Mum say no pets until after the move?"

"Yes, but if there's a kitten right here,

needing a home..."

They both looked towards the bush. Alice's heart ached.

"Hmm," said Grandma, thoughtfully. "Gypsy's obviously a happy cat, she looks well-fed. The kittens may already have homes to go to... But I'll ask around, see if anyone knows who's having them."

"And remember we're not telling anyone about the rose garden!" added Alice.

"Right," said Grandma. "It's a butterfly sanctuary, probably," she said, looking around at the wilderness. "I expect they've left it alone on purpose."

They lifted the creeper carefully and squeezed back out through the gate, leaving everything as it was. Alice had a last look around, to see if she could

see the cat again, but there was no sign
of her.

"So, um, Mum," said Alice, later that
evening. "Did I mention that Gypsy
has kittens?"

"Hmm?" said Mum. "Gypsy who?"

"The park cat, the one Grandma and
I met today."

"Lovely, darling."

Mum wasn't really listening. She was
sorting out piles of old clothes, books and
toys, stacking them in boxes, ready for the
charity shop.

"So when are we moving again, Mum?"

Her mother put down the box she was
carrying. She put her arm around Alice
and rumpled her hair. They both looked
across at the calendar on the wall, where

Alice was ticking off the weeks with a red pen. "Not long now," she said. "Just two more months to go."

Alice groaned. Two months! That seemed forever away.

She couldn't wait to move house – she'd have a much bigger bedroom, and Mum would have a study to work in. They'd have a garden of their own, too. Alice could carry on going to the same school when they moved, and best of all, the new house was still only a slightly longer bus ride away from Grandma's, in the other direction. So she and Grandma would still be able to have adventures together.

At this thought, Alice returned to the idea that was preoccupying her.

"And also... Mum?"

"Hmm?" Alice's mother was bent over her sorting task again.

"Mum-a?" Her mother looked up and raised an eyebrow. They both knew that Alice only ever called her 'Muma' when she was asking for something. "Yes, darling. What is it?"

"We're allowed pets at the new house, aren't we?"

"Alice Allen! Do you ever give up?" Mum was laughing.

"No," said Alice. "I never do."

16

Chapter Two

It was wild and windy that night.

Gypsy was clever enough to make sure
her family was well hidden under a big,
broken old pot, propped up against the
wall behind the curtain of ivy. Nobody
would ever guess they were there. Except
the little girl and the old lady who had
visited earlier in the day – but they had
gone away again.

She licked the kittens with her rough tongue until they squeaked. She lay back and watched them clamber about in the dark.

All three kittens had milky eyes that were still tight-shut, and their little ears were still flat against their heads. The two black boy kittens were strong, already trying to push themselves up on their out-sized paws, and mewing loudly. They would be alright. The little grey tabby kitten was much smaller than the boys. But more worrying was that she didn't seem very awake. She was hardly moving. As Gypsy watched, one of the boys blundered into the little grey girl and trod on her, and she opened her tiny pink mouth and gave a strong squeak of protest. Then she too tried to teeter upright, almost managing it...and Gypsy let herself relax.

Outside, the gate swung on its hinges: open, shut, rattle, slam. Rain lashed against the old wall and streamed down onto the clay pot roof, but it held. They were warm and dry. Gypsy was still very tired. Gently, she picked up her wobbly kittens in her mouth, one by one, and tucked them in under her.

Then she fell asleep.

A scrawny fox scrambled up onto the wall and paused, lifting his nose to test the air, his whiskers twitching. He smelt fresh earth and damp leaves. He heard the rain *ping-pinging* steadily on the clay pot, but its rhythmic *drip-dripping* drowned out the delicate *meeiou-meeiou* call of the kittens. Using his bushy tail to balance, the fox turned, jumped back down from the wall and trotted away, towards the interesting smell of an upturned bin, blown over by the wind.

Gypsy dozed. Three tiny kittens tottered blindly back and forth over her folded paws, butting their blunt heads into her side and mewing, until she stirred. They were hungry. She nudged them in closer to her, so they could suckle. Snuggled up together, safe and snug, Gypsy and her kittens snoozed all night.

Alice had hardly slept, listening to the blustery night, and wondering how Gypsy would cope. After school, she sped through her homework.

"Can I go over to the park and check on the kittens?"

"Yes, I should think so," said Mum. "But I'm not sure Gypsy will let you anywhere near them – be careful not to frighten her."

"Yes, mum, I promise," said Alice.

The last thing Alice wanted was to scare Gypsy. She wanted to help, if she could. Gypsy was used to taking care of herself, but now she had the kittens to worry about, too! The summer was over, and the autumn nights were getting much colder. Alice hated to think of the cat family sleeping rough. The new mother would be guarding the kittens, and that might mean she needed food. Perhaps Alice could take her a warm blanket, and something to keep off the rain.

She raced over to the park, ducking under the ivy and slipping through the creaky gate.

Red and gold leaves whirled down from the trees and danced all around her. She sat on the wet bench, arms wrapped around her folded up legs, chin on her knees. Wispy clouds scudded across the sky. The trees rustled, a gathering wind swirled the leaves on the ground, and Alice knew she should be getting home.

But she wanted to see Gypsy and the kittens.

Before long, a cat came padding out of the bushes, and sat in front of her, a safe distance away.

"Hello, Gypsy." Alice slid down off the bench and crouched down, holding out her hand. "Did you manage to keep out of the rain last night?"

But the little cat glared at her, as if to say, *I'm busy here!* and turned to disappear into the dense undergrowth.

Alice didn't mind. She could hear the kittens squeaking – they needed their mother. And Gypsy wasn't an ordinary house cat – she couldn't be expected to suddenly make friends, like any old tabby! Especially when she had newborn kittens to protect. And Gypsy seemed to have everything under control. Alice felt quite sure the kittens were warm and dry.

She sat for a while longer, hugging her knees, listening to the kittens, wondering what they looked like. Then she got up and picked her way back across the garden. Before she left, she carefully rearranged the dangling ivy, to make sure the gate stayed hidden. She walked home, humming happily under her breath, kicking up the leaves.

Alice went back to the garden whenever she could over the next few weeks, but there was no sign of the kittens. She was beginning to wonder whether they were in trouble. She consulted Grandma.

"It's normal for kittens to stay hidden when they're so vulnerable," said Grandma. "It means Gypsy is being very cautious. She's obviously a very good mother."

Of course she is, thought Alice proudly. She couldn't help thinking of Gypsy as *her* cat, even though she knew it wasn't really true. Still, every time she went to visit, Gypsy did take a break from bringing up her kittens to emerge from the bushes to say hello, in her reserved, wild-cat way. Alice felt sure Gypsy was beginning to trust her.

"So when do you think Gypsy will bring

them outside?" she asked. She and Mum were moving in exactly four weeks. She couldn't even think about leaving before seeing the kittens.

"Let's see," said Grandma. Alice heard a clunk as Grandma put down the phone, and a papery rustle as she looked in her book.

"For the first couple of days she's got to keep them warm, and just let them suckle and sleep. But their eyes will be open now; they open after about a week."

So they could see!

"And will they be standing up?"

"Oh yes, they'll be moving about," said Grandma. "They'll be twice the size they were at birth."

Alice thought about that for a moment. She tried to imagine how big the kittens had been when she and Grandma found them. They had probably been just a few days old – it was very difficult to say – Gypsy had hidden them so well. They'd probably have been about as long as my finger, she said to herself, so now they'd be the length of my hand.

"After about a month, I'd say, we might catch a glimpse of them," said Grandma.

"It's been at least a month since that first day when we heard them crying," she added. "Let's see. They were fairly newborn then…"

Grandma was trying to work out how old the kittens were. "Yes, they'll definitely be over a month old now," she said, finally.

Alice was so excited, she nearly dropped the phone. She thanked Grandma and promised to keep her updated. Grandma was almost as excited about the kittens as she was. And she was on Alice's side, too, about getting a kitten of her own.

Alice grabbed her coat. There was just time to fit in a visit before supper!

Chapter Three

Gypsy's kittens were strong and fit, and their little fur coats were thick and fluffy. Grandma was right – they were over a month old, and they were ready for solid food. Their mother would need to leave them for longer periods to hunt for park rats, and fish for tasty leftover tuna sandwiches in the bins.

But first she needed to teach them how to fend for themselves.

Gypsy squeezed out from under the old pot and called them, with low, reassuring growls, to follow.

After a pause, two sets of pointy black ears appeared in the shadowy gap under the pot. It was the two boys. They shot boldly out into the wiry mesh of trunks and branches, but they stopped short where the shadowy rose bushes ended and the tall grasses began, mewing for their mother. She nudged them on and out, and that's when Grandma and Alice, sitting quietly on the bench, were rewarded with their first proper sighting.

"Grandma, look!" whispered Alice. Two wobbly kittens emerged, blinking, from the undergrowth. They were jet black, but their paws were white. *They look like they're wearing socks*, thought Alice.

And they had little patches of white on their chests, like shirt fronts. She was so excited she nearly jumped up, but at the last minute she remembered not to make any sudden movements.

Grandma squeezed her hand. They sat together, perfectly still.

It was dusk, and the light was dimming fast. The swaying trees made a silvery, shimmery sound all around them. Gypsy needn't have chosen this moment to bring her kittens out, Alice thought, happily. It was almost as though she were showing them off, introducing them.

"Now wait a minute," said Grandma. "Is there one more?"

With perfect timing, a third fluffy streak burst out of the rose bushes and skittered suddenly to a halt, startling her two

brothers. They bolted back under the
bushes to their mother, with their ears
back. The tiny grey kitten patted at a leaf
on the ground with her paw. *Grrr, ssss!*
She spat bravely at the leaf, and puffed her
tail up. Then she spun around to snatch at
another twirling leaf behind her, twisted
in midair and landed awkwardly, stiff-
legged. She froze...and then galloped off
again, crashing back through the long
grass and out of sight.

It was too funny – Alice let out a strangled giggle. Next to her, Grandma's shoulders shook, and she wiped her eyes.

"She's a feisty one," she said. "Got a lot of her mother in her. Did you see those pretty tabby markings?"

"She's so sweet, isn't she?" said Alice.

"Yes, she is. Such a dainty little girl," said Grandma. "I think their father must be a grey tabby. There's a big grey that lives on the other side of the park. I often stop and talk to him."

All the kittens knew they would be finding new owners soon, and so they were on their best behaviour. Gypsy helped them revise all the cat-skills they needed to master before they could leave home. Under her watchful eye, they spent diligent hours climbing and tumbling, spitting and scratching, stalking and pouncing. The boy kittens worked hard at learning how to be proper cats. When they were eight weeks old, Gypsy was satisfied that they were ready. She had the perfect owner in mind for each of them.

She led her oldest boy across the park to Mrs Watson's house, and up the stone steps. She licked him all over, until he was clean and tidy. He sat up proudly, claws

38

tucked in, tufty fur smoothed down, his creamy front bib soft and fluffy, looking exactly as though his mother had combed him and done up his top button! Gypsy butted her kitten gently on the forehead, before retreating back across the road. She jumped up onto the park fence and turned to watch him. A young, shiny black crow flapped down to perch on the fence near her, head on one side, watching and waiting, too.

Remembering to look as adorable as possible, her kitten mewed as loudly as he could. The door opened. Gypsy heard a delighted cooing and a clucking, and saw her boy leaning and rubbing up against the little old lady's legs. Mrs Watson scooped the purring kitten up into her arms, and carried him inside.

For her second boy, Gypsy chose the Taylor family at number 42. The two young Taylor children often stopped to talk to Gypsy on their walks in the park, and she knew they had no cat of their own at home. She nuzzled and licked her dusty kitten until his black fur shone, and tidied up his ears. He cleaned his paws and straightened his whiskers all by himself, like the grown-up kitten he was.

Picking him up gently just behind his head, Gypsy propped him on the windowsill and waited below. The little kitten looked admiringly at himself in the reflection for a moment. He sat up straight, tucked in his tail neatly as his mother had taught him, lifted one paw to tap on the glass, and gave a loud mew.

Waiting under the
deep ledge, Gypsy
heard the muffled
sound of the
children calling
their dad to come
quickly! She
heard the
window open.

"Hello there, little
guy. Where did you
come from?"

As her boy launched into a rumbling
purr, a head poked out and looked about
for a moment. The little kitten was lifted
up and in.

"I think he's a hungry little kitten,"
Gypsy heard next, floating out of the
open window. "We may have a tin of tuna

somewhere. How would you like that?"

Satisfied, Gypsy padded away and down the front steps.

Soon, it would be her youngest, little grey's turn. Gypsy lay draped along the red brick wall, in a warm patch of late autumn sun. One large front paw dangling, she looked down at her last kitten, who was playing with her friend, the gleaming, blue-black crow. She was certainly brave...the bird was three times her size! He stopped to poke about in his feathers with his beak; inching along behind him, the little kitten stopped too. He swivelled his head to look at her with a beady eye. It was as though he was daring her to catch him!

Caw-caw! The kitten flopped down on her side, and licked a paw. The crow

turned to walk on again – a peculiar
lurching high step, tail feathers pointing
down stiffly. The kitten got up and trailed
him. She crouched down, her tail
whipping, ready to pounce...and just as
she launched herself at him, the crow
flapped off. He sat on the wall and
laughed down at
her, *caw-caw!*

Gypsy's kitten
turned her back
on him huffily,
and sat up primly,
tucking her tiny
fluffy tail in, cleverly
managing to make just the
very tip of it twitch,
crossly. Coping
with an unruly tail

was one of the most difficult things for a kitten to learn, and little grey was doing very well, her mother noted, as she looked on with a critical eye.

What sort of home would suit her naughtiest, cleverest kitten? Gypsy gave a lazy yawn – she was not worried at all. She knew a solution would present itself. She got up and stretched, claws out, back arched. She picked her way daintily along the wall, her long tail curled into a question mark.

The last little kitten wasn't worried about finding a home, either. She was too busy practising the most difficult cat skill of all – climbing. Concentrating hard, she put her claws out and stretched as high as she could. Sticking her bottom out and using her tail to help her balance, she shimmied and shuffled her way up through a twisty rose bush. She emerged at the top, looking very pleased with herself.

"Well done!" Alice called from her bench. The kitten didn't stop there – she jumped, over and up, onto the high wall. She teetered, and turned wobbily around to miaow to Alice, *look at me!* But she had forgotten how narrow the old wall was. Her bottom slipped off, and she swung for a moment, managing to cling on by her front paws, scrabbling at the bricks with her back legs, and mewing, *help!*

Further along the wall, Gypsy turned back to help, but Alice got there first.

She jumped up and scrambled across the tangled garden.

"You poor little thing, you were doing so well!"

She reached up to detach the kitten's needle-sharp claws from the crumbly bricks, and lifted her down. The little kitten nestled into the crook of Alice's arm, purring.

She looked up at Alice smiling down at her, and her tiny body vibrated, as she revved up like an engine, and then launched into a rumbling purr. She wriggled around so she could stand up in Alice's arms. She put

46

both her paws up to Alice's shoulders, and butted her under the chin. Alice tickled her between her ears, and the little kitten sighed happily.

"I'll talk to Mum tonight," Alice promised her.

Gypsy looked down at them. Her little grey had chosen a new owner all by herself! It was a very good match, reflected Gypsy, watching the little girl cuddle her kitten. She turned to continue weaving along the wall, looking for another sunny spot where she could toast her tummy on the warmed bricks.

47

Chapter Four

It was Alice's mum who raised the subject of the little grey kitten first.

"Grandma tells me that old Mrs Watson has decided to take one of the park kittens," she said, casually buttering a piece of toast. "She says the Taylors are having one, too. And apparently there's just one left, all on her own."

Alice scanned her mother's face

anxiously – she couldn't tell what was coming next.

"Do you think..." she said, very carefully, "there's any way we could have her?"

"Well, quite possibly," said Mum. "Grandma did mention it to me the other day. And I *have* been thinking about it. In fact I went down to *Paws* while you were at school today." *Paws* was the pet shop Alice regularly dragged Mum to, on the pretext of looking at the rabbits and mice, but really, to drop hints about kittens.

"What did you buy, Mum?" said Alice. She could hardly believe she was actually having the conversation she had imagined so often. And it was going just as she'd dreamed it would.

"Well, I bought this..." Her mother

opened the cupboard behind her, and pulled out a cat basket.

"Oh, and this..." She opened the basket and from inside, retrieved a pretty little collar.

"And not forgetting...this!" She pulled a sweet little mouse toy from her jeans pocket, and squeaked it at Alice. "So, what do you think?"

Alice had temporarily run out of words. She went to her mother, and put her arms around her.

"Thanks, Mum," she managed, after a long pause. "I can't believe it. Thanks so much. She's the cutest thing you've ever seen. You'll love her, you really will."

And then she gave a whoop, and ran to call Grandma.

A few short days later, Alice collected
Rosie from the park.

"I'll look after her so well, I promise,"
said Alice. "And I'll be able to come
and see you, when I come to stay at
Grandma's!" She tickled Gypsy under
the chin, and the mother cat rubbed noses
with her kitten through
the wide mesh of
the cat basket.
Then Gypsy gave
a little chirrup,
and turned to
vanish back into
the rose bushes,
her tail waving an elegant goodbye.

Alice took her little grey kitten home
and introduced her to Mum.

"Her name is Rosie," she announced.

"What a lovely name," said Mum. She was having a cuddle with Rosie while Alice puffed up the cushion in her basket. Until Rosie had learned how to use her litter tray, she was going to sleep in the kitchen. So Alice was making her a cosy den in the corner.

"Oh yes, that's perfect!" said Grandma. She had come round to welcome Rosie home.

"It's because we found her in a rose garden," explained Alice.

Miaow! said Rosie, in-between purrs, from Mum's arms.

"I definitely think she approves of her new name," said Mum.

Alice put Rosie's mouse toy and a teddy from Grandma into the basket and Mum put Rosie gently down on the cushion.

53

The little kitten purred and pushed and pulled at the soft padding, her tiny paw-pads spread and her claws out. Then she turned herself around several times, before curling up in a little fluffy ball, as close as possible to her new teddy.

It had been a long day. As her new family peered down at her, she gave a little yawn, and a dozy, squeaky *mi*– and fell fast asleep.

Like all conscientious mother cats, Gypsy had toilet-trained her kittens early, showing them how to keep their clay-pot shelter clean and dry. So it only took Rosie a day to work out how to use the litter tray. Then she was allowed to sleep with Alice, waking her up early for school every morning by tramping up and down the bed, forgetting to pull her claws in and tripping over, and then mewing loudly for her breakfast.

Every morning Alice kissed her goodbye and then Rosie spent the day with Mum, waiting for her to get back from school. While Mum worked in the living room, Rosie hunted flies behind the sofa, and practised sharpening her claws on the backs of the chairs, when Mum wasn't looking.

Sometimes Rosie's friend, the crow, flapped over from the park to visit. He sat on the windowsill, and Rosie sat on the back of the sofa and pressed her nose to the glass, and told him all about her new family.

Rosie loved Mum. After she caught Rosie practising her cat-climbing skills on the curtains, Mum moved the kitten's basket next to her desk so she could keep an eye on her. Then Rosie cried to be picked up, and slept, curled up on Mum's lap, while she worked. She followed Mum into the kitchen to ask for fishy treats, whenever she went to make a cup of tea.

When Alice had homework to do Rosie sat on her lap and tried to help – but she could never resist getting up and tramping across the keys, batting Alice's funny clicky 'mouse' with her paw, and then flinging herself down onto her side, scattering loose paper and knocking books out of the way.

"Rosie! Try and focus!" said Alice, tickling her fluffy tummy. But Rosie just rolled onto her back, purring happily, and wondering how on earth Alice had ever managed homework without her.

Alice's mother was very strict about not letting Rosie go outside yet. It was too soon. Rosie might go too far and get confused, and not be able to find her way back. But more importantly, the move was happening in Rosie's first week with the Allen family, so Mum wanted to wait, and let Rosie explore the *new* house and garden.

The day before the move, Alice still had to go to school. She tried to persuade Mum that she needed to be at home to help, but her mother was immoveable.

"It'll be chaos, crates everywhere," she said. "I can't have you underfoot, too. Honestly, you're better off going to school. It's just one more day."

"But what about Rosie? Who's going to look after her?"

"I will," said Mum.

"But she might think she's being left behind if I disappear now," protested Alice. "And all the noise might upset her..."

They both looked down at Rosie. She was stalking a scrap of polystyrene foam behind an empty packing case, oblivious to the kerfuffle around her. She crouched, wiggling her bottom to make her tail

58

sweep back and forth. *Grrr! Ssss!* She pounced, sat up, chewed on her catch for a moment and then spat it out, yuck, looking disgusted. *She doesn't exactly look anxious*, thought Alice, as her adorable kitten padded away, holding her tail straight up like an exclamation mark. She looked more like a miniature version of her wild-cat mother.

"She'll be fine," said Mum, ushering Alice to the door.

Early next morning, Alice got out of bed and went to look out of the window for the last time – she would miss her view of the park. But on this last day, the sky was overcast, and the air crackled with thunder. Bare branches whipped in the wintery wind. Brown and red leaves flew around on the ground.

Rosie woke up with her fur tingling. Mum and Alice were having their breakfast, but Rosie felt too excited to eat. She skittered across the kitchen, chasing her mouse. She tried to stop, but skidded on her bottom, crashing into the kitchen cupboard. She scrambled up and pushed off again, spinning like a top on the shiny floor, trying and failing to brake with her front paws.

"What *is* Rosie doing?" Alice spluttered, choking on her juice.

"Oh, sweetie, she's gone all scatty," said Mum. "I don't know why, but all cats go a little crazy when there's a storm brewing."

"Even wild cats," said Alice. She scooped Rosie up onto her knee, but Rosie wriggled to get down.

After breakfast Rosie was shut in the kitchen, because, as Alice explained, it was dangerous for her to be getting under the removal men's feet. She might get trodden

61

on! She had her basket and her mouse and her teddy, and a bowl of delicious fishy biscuits, but she was far too excited to feel hungry, and she certainly wasn't sleepy. She pressed her nose to the crack of light in the kitchen door and smelled the cardboard boxes and wooden crates, and listened to the clump and thump of heavy furniture being carried down the stairs, and the friendly hum of the removal men's voices. She scratched at the door and mewed, until Alice came and said, "Sssh, Rosie! Or we'll have to take you to Grandma's!"

Rosie definitely didn't want to go to Grandma's. She wanted to stay here with Alice. She trotted back to her basket and curled up. She was going to try her best to be a good kitten, and wait quietly for Alice to come and see her, and perhaps then she might be allowed to join in.

The kitchen door creaked open, and she saw Mum's legs, and heard her saying, "More tea? Was it two sugars...and milk?"

The door was ajar. Rosie spotted a packing-crate on its side, full of little wiggly white mice. Mice! She lost her wild-kitten head, forgot all her good-kitten resolutions, and caterpaulted herself through the narrowing gap, as the door swung shut.

Chapter Five

Rosie bolted across the living room and dived behind the curtains. Nobody noticed her. She peeped out and took in the hustle-bustle of the room, her blue eyes as big as saucers, and shining with excitement. Her whiskers quivered as she read the air for signals – just like a big cat would! Her nose twitched – the room was full of mixed-up, interesting smells. But she could tell them all apart, she thought proudly. She could smell sweat – that was the removal men, working hard, wrapping things up and dragging furniture around. She could smell the paper being wrapped around breakable precious things and padding out the crates – that was old newspapers. There was the musty smell of cobwebs and dust, freshly disturbed and swirling up behind chairs that hadn't been moved for years. And that lovely familiar, sweet-clean-shampoo smell...was Alice. From behind the curtain Rosie spotted Alice's stripey socks; she was kneeling down, helping Mum wrap up the glasses.

Perhaps, thought Rosie, she wouldn't call out to Alice just yet. She wanted to see what was going on first. She was safe here behind the curtain, and in a moment she would nip back to her basket. It was lovely that Alice was trying to look after her, but really, she was being a bit too protective. Rosie was a wild-cat after all – she could look after herself!

Rosie's view from her hiding place was limited to feet and crates and cardboard boxes. She decided to get a better view of all the action. She stood up on her hind legs, dug her front claws into the draped curtain lining, and climbed. The curtain swayed dangerously as she progressed vertically on the inside of it, using her tail to balance, ripping and tearing her way up, pulling her claws out and re-inserting them, half-wishing Alice could see her and half-hoping she couldn't because really, Rosie did know that climbing curtains and chairs was not allowed. Not at all.

Halfway up she heard a box drop with a *thump!* which made her jump, the curtain twisting as she clung on and spun... She was just wondering how she was going to get untangled and climb down again when, with a loud ripping sound, the lining tore altogether. With her front claws still attached but her hind legs scrabbling, bottom out, she plummeted back down to the ground. She crash-landed – extremely painfully and inelegantly – and scrambled upright. Success! Her bottom throbbed, and above her ears, the lining hung in tatters. But Rosie didn't care – she had climbed all the way up a curtain, and slid back down again! With a happy sigh, she shook her front paws, to get rid of the thin ribbons of torn curtain. She was very glad nobody had seen her undignified descent.

But had they heard her? She peered out again from behind the curtain, holding her breath. She was in luck. Above the noisy crashing and banging of packing, nobody had heard a thing!

69

Her hiding place was full of little transparent spiders with spindly legs, and Rosie pounced on one or two, but they darted away, and their dusty cobwebs caught in her whiskers and made her sneeze. It was very warm behind the curtain, next to the radiator... She gave a yawn. Perhaps she might head back to her basket now, she thought, sleepily. She was still little enough to need lots of naps, and climbing curtains was tiring work. But just as she was eyeing the kitchen door, and wondering when it would swing open again, she spotted the tipped-over packing case, full of wiggly white mice. Her heart began to beat again, and she sunk down low, into a hunting crouch.

Nobody saw her scoot out from behind the curtain and into the crate, scattering

70

squiggly polystyrene foam beads. Nobody noticed her realising her mistake, scrabbling frantically backwards on her bottom, twisting onto her front, just too late, as the crate was hauled upright, showering her with white foam beads... Hidden in the gap at the top of the packing-case, Rosie looked up as the looming lid came down and blocked out the light. She opened her mouth to mew, *wait! stop!*...but instead she heard herself make a terrified little squeak. She had lost her miaow! A second later, she managed a croak. But it was drowned out by the *bam-bam* of a hammer, as the crate was nailed shut.

Then Rosie felt a jolt. She heard a grunt, *oof*, as her packing case was lifted up, and then she felt herself tip, and sway, and heard the *clump-thump* of steps on the stairs.

Miaow-miaow-miaow! Help! called Rosie, lying on her back like a beetle, her voice muffled under the lid. She heard footsteps *crunch-crunching*, then a crash, as the packing case was righted again. She heard a *slide*, and a *slam*...and then, an awful silence. She was all on her own in the dark!

Rosie crouched under the lid of the packing case, breathing little panicky shallow breaths, and wondering what to do. She felt her crate judder. She listened to the crashes and bangs as other boxes were loaded into the van around hers.

She closed her eyes and tried to imagine that she was tucked up in her cosy basket with her teddy, and Alice hovering nearby, about to give her one of those tasty fishy snacks.

Thinking about Alice calmed Rosie down. Eventually Mum would realise what had happened, wouldn't she? And Alice would rescue her...she just had to wait. It had been a long, eventful day for the little kitten. The cramped space under the lid of the crate was warm and dark. She felt her eyes droop...and had almost dozed off when the van engine woke up and growled. The back of the van was filled with a loud chugging noise, but Rosie could still hear the faint sound of voices outside the van. *Miaow-miaow-miaow!* she mewed frantically, lying on her side, scratching at the wooden lid. *Alice, help!* But if it was Alice standing outside the van, she couldn't hear her kitten crying. Rosie's crate lurched and shuddered. She shrank down and braced herself, as she felt the van move off.

Trapped inside the packing crate amongst the loose white foam beads, Rosie was jolted and bounced as the van rumbled along. Every time it turned a corner her crate slid and knocked into the others, and she was thrown around inside it. Rounding a particularly sharp bend in the road, the van tipped, her packing crate rocked...and then toppled over completely. *Slam!* Rosie was thrown onto her back again. Spitting out a mouthful of foam, she twisted over. Craning her neck to look behind her, she saw a thin crack of light. The lid had been loosened! Pushing and kicking with her back legs, Rosie managed to make the gap wider. Now she had to worm and wriggle out backwards, trying to keep her tail tucked out of the way.

Wrenching and stretching her collar, so it almost slid up and over her head, Rosie backed her way out and onto the rattling floor of the van. She sat up shakily and – just for a moment, felt elated – she was free! But the van turned another corner, and with a loud groan, all the heavy furniture in the van began sliding over towards her. Rosie scrambled to get up onto one of the moving boxes, and out of the way. She mewed desperately, and tried to dive back into *her* half-open crate, but it shifted and twisted away... High in the van she zig-zagged desperately from crate to crate, leaping towards the one thing she recognised – the sofa. She scrambled down onto it and cowered under a cushion, digging in her claws, as the sofa rocked back and forth. Shaking like a leaf,

her ears back and her eyes squeezed shut, Rosie mewed frantically for the noise to stop, for Alice to come and help her.

And then...she heard the loud squeal of brakes. The van lurched to a halt, slamming the sofa up against the inside wall. The clattering engine complained for a bit longer, then shuddered into silence.

Thud-thud... Rosie's heart thumped in her chest. The blood thrummed and sang in her ears. *Crunch-crunch-crunch* – an unmistakeable sound broke the silence. It was the sound of boots on gravel. Rosie shrank down under her cushion and blinked, as the door slid open and light streamed in.

"Right, darling," said Alice's mother. They stood in the road and watched the van rumble away and out of sight.

A crow sat hunched on the park fence like a folded umbrella, watching them. As raindrops began to patter down, he half-opened his wings and sidled along the fence and called out to them, *caw!*

"I think he's telling us about the storm," said Mum, wrapping her cardigan tightly around her and looking up at the darkening sky.

"Oh, that's Charlie," said Alice. "That's what I call him anyway. He's sort of friends with Gypsy and he plays with her kittens. It's really sweet!"

Caw! The crow said at this, and flapped away.

"Well, *he's* got the right idea!" said Mum. "Let's get in out of the rain. Let's have a drink, and what about a chocolate biscuit?"

Alice nodded. Even though she really did want to move closer to Grandma, and she really did want a bigger bedroom, she was feeling a bit wobbly about leaving the flat. It was strange to think she might never come here again. "Can Rosie ride in the front with me?"

"Of course she can. Let's go up and give her the run of the empty flat, before she goes in her cat basket."

The prospect of taking Rosie with her to the new house made Alice feel much better. She trailed up the stairs behind her mother, absent-mindedly wondering what Rosie would make of having her very own cat flap, and humming under her breath – she always hummed when she was happy. But as her mother swung open the kitchen door she stopped abruptly, so that Alice, who was right behind, banged into her.

"That's odd..." They both stared down at the empty basket.

"Where is she?"

Alice and her mother walked around the empty flat, calling Rosie's name. They searched everywhere it was possible for a small kitten to hide in a small flat – which wasn't very many places, since all the furniture had gone, and all that was left was their little pile of bags.

Rosie simply wasn't there, and Alice felt a shivery spike of fear."Mum, where is she? What's happened to her?" she said.

Mum looked puzzled, "I really don't understand it," she said slowly. She was rewinding the events of the day in her head. "Did we leave the kitchen door open just now? Or at any point? I don't think we did... Did we?"

"What if she got out of the flat? She could have run outside! Into the road!" Alice grabbed her coat.

"But...then how did she get out of the kitchen?" said her mother, looking mystified. She rooted through her bag to

81

find her mobile. "Perhaps she somehow did though, and managed to get into one of the crates... Let's call the removals company and get hold of the van driver."

"Into a *crate*? Oh no...poor Rosie," said Alice. She dropped her coat and sank down in a heap. "She's just a baby. She'll be so scared!"

"Yes, but *if* that's what's happened, the main thing is, she'll still be in there, and she'll be safe," said her mother, soothingly. "We'll call them, and if they don't have her, we'll go outside and look for her. Don't worry darling. We'll find her. She can't have gone far." With the phone to her ear, she stood looking out of the window at the swaying treetops. The rain was bucketing down now and it would be dark soon. She very much hoped that Rosie *had* somehow got into a crate and was still in the van. It was not a good night for any kitten to be lost and alone outside.

Chapter Six

You're not Alice, thought Rosie, shakily. She had just narrowly escaped being squashed – she wasn't going to risk being caught by a strange man. So she hunkered down, making herself as invisible as she could.

"Hmm, thought so," grumbled the van driver. "Everything's come loose. We'll have to strap it all down again."

He slid the van door wider and stepped heavily up into it, making the ramshackle towers of crates and furniture rock, and teeter.

"Er...Dave!" he turned to call out in alarm. "Quick, give us a hand, will you? It's all about to come down!" He put out a hand to steady an overhanging box, and a foot to brace himself.

In the gloom at the back of the van, Rosie inched forward, her whiskers testing the fresh air. Alice was out there somewhere. And she was going to find her. She gathered herself to make a dash for it, but something yanked her back. It was her collar buckle, snagged on the loose sofa cover. She pulled forwards, and backwards, and shook her head frantically. But she was stuck. Her heart pounding, she stopped struggling. Lying on her side instead, and putting her ears down flat against her head, she tucked in her chin, braced all four paws against the back of the sofa and wriggled backwards. Leaving the collar where it was, she jumped lightly down on to the van floor and scooted behind a crate. The man stood with his back to her, silhouetted in the doorway. Beyond him, Rosie could see a grey curtain of rain. It was drumming loudly on the outside of the van.

"Oh no," tutted Dave, taking in the sight of the almost-toppling crates and his friend, struggling to hold them up, both legs splayed and arms spreadeagled.

"Er, Dave, I could use some help here," muttered his friend, teeth gritted, sweating furiously.

Dave heaved a weary sigh. All the crates would have to come out. Look at that, one of them had fallen over and the lid was loose... As he pulled himself up into the van, his mobile began to ring. Twisting to pull it out of his pocket, he failed to notice the tiny grey kitten flitting past him like a ghost.

Rosie cowered under a car, her wet fur flattened against her tiny body. Water streamed in rivulets across the uneven concrete all around her. If only she had listened to Alice, she thought miserably, she would be at home in the kitchen right now, curled up in her basket. It was so dark and misty she could barely see the van, and the men dragging all the boxes out, opening them up, and peering in. It was so cold...and she couldn't see Alice anywhere. Should she get back in the van?

Just as this thought occurred to her, the men slammed the doors and jumped back in. The van coughed and spluttered, and she watched it sloosh away across the water-logged car park. Rosie's teeth chattered; she shivered and ached with tiredness.

89

She couldn't just sit under here in the middle of this enormous puddle. But what was she going to do? And how was she ever going to find Alice, all by herself in the middle of a storm?

A loud flap-fluttering interrupted her gloomy thoughts. She gave herself a shake, and sat up. *Caw... Caw?* She saw a pair

of stick-thin poker-straight legs, and then a pair of bright eyes, peering sideways at her. *Caw?*

Miaow! she said, feeling a rush of hope. It was her crow!

She padded forward to say hello. *Charlie! Where's Alice?*

Caw! said Charlie. And he flew away.

Rosie dived out from under the car just as another roared past, drenching her with a great slew of freezing water. She looked wildly around for Charlie. An icy wind gusted straight at her, almost blowing her off her feet. Making one last gigantic effort, she put her head down and her ears back, and ran blindly across the road.

Alice's mother put her arm around her.

"I've spoken to the men, and they've actually just stopped, and they're going to search the van for her now. So don't worry darling. If she's in there, they'll find her."

"But what if they're really loud, and they frighten her?"

"No, no," said Mum. "I told them to be really careful, and they will be. While we're waiting for them to call back let's check the park. If Rosie *did* manage to get out of the flat, she might just have tried to make her way back to her mother..."

But there was no Rosie in the secret garden. Just Gypsy, sheltering from the rain under a bench. She came out to greet Alice, sniffing her hand and leaning against her legs. *She trusts me*, Alice thought miserably. She, Alice, had promised Gypsy faithfully that she would look after her kitten. And look what had happened...

"I'm sorry, Gypsy," she whispered. "I'll find her. I will."

Grandma was waiting at the flat.

"That was the removals men. They're at the new house and they've unloaded the van," she said. "Darling, I'm sorry. They haven't found Rosie. But they've got her collar."

"Her collar?" Alice's voice wobbled. "So she was in the van..."

"Yes," said Mum, walking back to the window and looking out at the angry sky. The rain was turning to icy sleet. The wind was lashing against the glass. "But she isn't now."

"Oh no..." said Alice. "What do we do? We have to do something!"

"We need to look at a map," said Mum. "The van only stopped towards the end of the journey. So wherever Rosie is, she isn't far from her new home..."

"Wasn't that clever of her darling?" Grandma was wrapping Alice up in one of her comforting cuddles.

Alice didn't say anything. She couldn't. She was imagining her little kitten, out there somewhere, all on her own in the stormy night.

"Our best chance of finding her is to go over to the new house. We'll take a map, and look from there."

Grandma and Mum made a final tour of the empty flat. Picking up the last of the bags, Mum gave Grandma a look that Alice wasn't meant to see, and said something in a low voice Alice wasn't meant to hear either – but she did...

"It's lucky the van made just the one stop. But I'm afraid it was by the river."

By the river. *But kittens can't swim!* Tears dripped down Alice's nose.

"Well!" said Grandma, in an artificially cheery voice just in case Alice was listening, which she was. *She needn't bother*, thought Alice sadly. It didn't fool her one bit. "That doesn't necessarily mean she'll go down to the water!"

Alice brushed her tears away and sniffed, cross with herself for crying. Crying wasn't going to help Rosie. And in any case, she wouldn't need to go near the river. Would she?

Chapter Seven

Rosie was so relieved to be back home, so grateful for her cosy basket. She was *never* going exploring again, ever. From now on, she was going to be a good house-cat, not a naughty wild-cat. She helped Alice with her homework, and Alice said, "Rosie, I don't know how I ever managed to do this without you!" and then she sat on Alice's lap and watched television with

her, and it was lovely, except that the
television was very loud and thundery.

Alice stroked her behind the ears and
she purred, and then Alice picked her up,
and said, "What about one of those
delicious fishy snacks?" Rosie's empty
tummy protested so strongly at this, that
she half-woke up, and opened one bleary
eye. Too late, she squeezed it shut it again
and put both paws over her head, trying to
get back into her dream. But it faded away.

Everything came back with a rushing, sinking feeling that made her ears and whiskers droop. She couldn't go home – she was lost. She was all by herself in the dark night. She was hiding under a big, black bridge which dripped, but she had to stay there because there was a storm howling and crashing outside.

A swollen river was roaring and churning just a few feet below her muddy perch, and if she slipped, she would fall in and be carried away, and she would never see Alice again. And there were jittery shadows and scary night-time rustlings and scratchings, and she was waiting for Charlie. He had flown off to try and find out where Alice was.

And she was ravenous. She was starving to death!

Rosie sighed. She felt so faint, she could barely make the tip of her tail flick. But she managed a feeble twitch – it helped her think. She was so stiff, and cold, she needed a really good stretch. Then she gave herself a quick wash, all over, finishing by nibbling the dried mud out from between her claws, which made her feel much better. Now... she thought, as her tummy gave another painful rumble...

food. What would her mother do? She would go hunting, thought Rosie, that's what she'd do. But the rain was still hammering down outside, so Rosie couldn't go on a proper wild-cat expedition. She would have to hunt for scraps right here, in this enormous, echoey tunnel. So she sat up, and summoned up all her big-cat know-how.

She lifted her nose, and took a deep breath. Her nose twitched, and her whiskers trembled, and she scanned the dank night-time air. There had to be *something* she could eat.

Rosie could smell old shoe, and rusty metal, and soggy newspaper, and a pongy sock and mouldy plastic bags. High up in the shadowy, dripping arches, she could smell bat. And lurking somewhere, she picked up the stale stink of rat. She knew about rats from her mother, who hunted the ones that lived in the park. They were dangerous, and to be avoided at all costs. But there was something else. What was that tangy, salty smell?

Too hungry to be cautious, Rosie slid and slithered down the muddy bank to the water's edge. A half-unwrapped triangle of bread was caught in a branch, right next to the water's edge. A cheese sandwich!

Rosie knew all about fishing. She had seen her mother fish for leftover sandwiches in the park bins, hooking them out with her paw. Hunger made Rosie reckless. She leaned right out over the swirling water and swiped at the plastic triangle, scooping it out on her first go. She dragged her catch a little way and began to eat. She forgot to keep her ears pricked or her whiskers tuned in. And she turned her back on the source of the rat smell – the murky water. Which was not at all what her mother had taught her.

Fsss! The water rat lunged up out of the water, hissing and baring its chattering yellow teeth. Rosie shrank back, and the rat snatched at the sandwich.

But Rosie had not eaten for a very long time. She was not in the mood to let go of her supper. For just one second, she completely forgot that she was just a very damp, very tired kitten facing an enormous rodent with a nasty temper and huge, jagged teeth. *Grrr! Ssss!* She spat, and drew herself up, so that all her fur stood on end. Her tail whipped. *Miaow!* she said, *that's MINE!* And then she clouted the rat around the nose with her paw, remembering to extend all her claws.

It squealed with surprise, staggered and fell backwards into the river, floating away, clutching its bleeding muzzle. Rosie didn't even pause to celebrate. She was too busy polishing off every crumb of her cheese sandwich. When she had finished, Rosie licked her paws. She wished Alice could have seen her. She had found her own supper – and fought a rat for it!

The storm howled fiercely outside, and it was shivery and damp under the bridge. But with her tummy full, Rosie was feeling much more cheerful. She clambered back up to her ledge and curled up. She gave a yawn. Charlie would be back soon and then he would take her to Alice. While she was waiting, she needed to rest, and get her strength back. She closed her eyes, and let herself drift off to sleep.

While Rosie slept, the rain pelted down and the wind gathered strength. It tore branches off the trees and hurled them into the swollen river, which rose, higher and higher. When Rosie had been asleep for about an hour, the river burst its banks and boiled through the narrow bridge arch, carrying the storm debris with it. Rosie woke up just as a muddy wave washed over her. She tried to cling onto the bank, but her claws slipped on the mud. She let out a terrified wail, as she felt herself being swept away!

Alice was right. Rosie couldn't swim. But she tried to keep her face above the water, as the river spun her around. She flailed her paws and they scraped...something hard. It was a big

108

branch. She wrapped her front paws around it and pushed her chin up to the sky, and clung on. Her back legs and tail trailed behind her, and she squeezed her eyes shut. She scrabbled and clutched at the branch until both paws were numb. She opened her mouth and tried to mew for help, but she sputtered and choked on brown river water. Rosie knew she couldn't hold on much longer...then she felt a bump, and opened her eyes.

The branch had snagged on the muddy river bank; she was lying half-in and half-out of the shallows. But the water still tugged at Rosie's branch, trying to pull it away. She had to get out. Gathering all her reserves of strength, she dragged herself out and crawled as far up the bank as she could. She lay sprawled, gulping in air, waiting for her heart to slow down, and stop knocking painfully in her chest.

Icy rain pelted her. She lay there, willing herself on. If she thought she couldn't move, she was wrong. A flash of lightning and an angry thunderclap sent her scuttling higher up the grassy bank. At the top, she found a kind of wall, with half a roof on it. Another thunder-clap... and she dived in, looking for the tiniest space to squeeze herself into. She wedged herself into a corner. Dripping, shivering, Rosie looked around to see where she was.

"Remember Alice, this is Rosie," said Grandma. Tucking the umbrella under her arm, Alice tore off another strip of tape and handed it to her. Grandma stuck up the other corner of the poster and stood back to admire it. "She's no ordinary kitten," she added. "She's half wild-cat. And Gypsy will have trained her, too. She'll be somewhere nearby. It's just a matter of finding her." They were carrying a pile of 'lost kitten' posters. Alice had spent the morning lying on her new bedroom floor, making them. It was something constructive to do, apart from worrying.

LOST KITTEN
Grey and fluffy
Big blue eyes
Answers to the name of Rosie

REWARD!

Please call Alice Allen
0207

The reward was Rosie's idea. She had more than enough pocket money saved up to give to the amazing, kind person who rescued Rosie, and brought her back home.

She and Grandma had spent all afternoon

sticking up posters on lampposts in the wind and rain. They had put them up in the corner shop, and at the local vets. And they had tramped all around the streets near Alice's new house, knocking on doors, and asking people to please check their garden sheds, in case a little lost kitten might have got locked in by mistake.

But there was no sign of Rosie. Alice tried to keep positive, but she was very worried.

Rosie had been lost for a whole two days, and she had spent a whole night outside on her own. Mum was sure someone would have found her by now, and taken her in. But what if they hadn't? What if Rosie was still outside, all alone in the storm?

113

Chapter Eight

A pair of legs arrived, an umbrella was
shaken out with a *whoof*, and propped up
against the bench right in front of Rosie.
Muddy boots shuffled across her vision
and after a pause, she felt the bench
strain and creak above her. She heard
a grateful sigh, and a large canvas
shopping bag was plopped down next to
the half-open umbrella. She peered out

from between the boots and tried to work out where she was.

She was under a long bench, tucked under a simple awning. Rosie noticed that it was right by the side of the road, and as she watched, a very long bus pulled up. The doors sighed open, and several people shuffled off. With a scraping of gears, the bus coughed, and drove away.

I am at a bus stop, thought Rosie, feeling pleased with herself for knowing what that was. There had been a rubbish bin right next to the bus stop at the park gates. She had often hidden in the bushes with her mother, watching people getting on and off, lobbing their half-eaten lunch at the bin, unaware that they were providing an easy supper for a family of wild-cats.

Perhaps, thought Rosie, I can take the bus home?

But as she sat, and wondered, there was a flutter, and Charlie swooped down. He walked towards the bench, shaking out his wet wing feathers and re-folding them. *Caw*, he said. *Caw?*

Before a surprised Rosie had a chance to reply, a voice spoke from above her head.

"Hello there, Mr Crow," it said. "Aren't you a friendly boy! Now, what have I got for you here? Some crisps?" came the voice again, and a hand drifted down to rummage in the open shopping bag.

Rosie knew better than to speak. She didn't want to be found by this person, she wanted Alice. But Charlie took his chance, and sidled closer. He pecked at the crisps being scattered on the ground for him, and spoke to her, out of the side of his beak. *Caw-caw…caw!*

"Aren't you a talkative boy!" said the voice, as Charlie croaked. As Rosie listened her heart started beating faster, *bumpety-bumpety*, and her blue eyes shone.

After he had led Rosie to shelter under
the bridge, Charlie had flown up into the
storm and floated there, buffeted by the
rain and the wind, until his sharp eyes had
spotted the van, making its way to Rosie's
new house. He had followed the van, and
perched in a tree, watching the men
unloading. He had seen them carry the
sofa out onto the lawn, and discover
Rosie's collar, snagged behind the cushion.

And then Charlie had taken off to fly
back to Rosie. But high up in the storm,
he had been blown off course, and he had
lost his bearings. And he had been
searching for her ever since. He had
overheard the local pigeons gossiping
about the little kitten washed up by the
river – and they had directed him here,
to this bus shelter.

And there was something else, Charlie told her. Somehow, Rosie's adventure had brought her closer to home. Alice's new house was only a few streets away!

Rosie leapt up onto all four paws, her whiskers twitching. She was almost home! A bus pulled up, and the bench creaked, and the hand came down to pick up the shopping bag. And in a split second, Rosie made a decision. She was going home! She jumped into the shopping bag, and crouched down.

Caw! protested Charlie. But he could only watch helplessly, as the bag was lifted up and carried onto the bus with Rosie in it.

Stowed away under the seat, Rosie shook and rattled along, amongst the shopping in the bag. The roar and heat of the bus bore down on her, and she opened her mouth in a silent mew of despair. She'd made a mistake. How ever would she get off this bus, and how would she find Alice?

Ting-ting-ting! With a juddering shriek of brakes, the bus stopped again. From her shopping bag, Rosie saw the doors sigh open. She bolted. Weaving between shoes and boots, and bags, she galloped towards the door as it sighed again, and the gap began to close. Rosie shot out onto the pavement, and landed in a heap.

She was out. But where was she?

An old Labrador ambled down the street, some way behind his owner. His daily walk took him past the same landmarks every day, and he enjoyed smelling them all. He checked his lamppost, and his favourite bush. No change there. At the bus stop, his nose told him about the trembling kitten, hiding under the bench. He bent down and snuffled a greeting. But Rosie didn't reply, she hung her head. She had learnt her lesson. She was staying where she was, and waiting for Charlie to come and find her.

The grizzly old boy mosied along, slowly catching up with his owner, wondering all the while where he had seen that kitten before. Just as his owner was about to clip his lead back on, the old dog remembered. He had seen her picture on a lamppost. He turned and trotted all the way back to the bus shelter, as his startled owner puffed along behind him.

Woof! barked the old dog. He was telling Rosie to follow him.

I can't, mewed Rosie, with a tiny voice.

Woof-woof! said the dog again, adding a whine to emphasise his point, and wagging his tail. And Rosie thought she heard him say, *Alice! Alice?* Rosie's ears pricked, and she looked up, and listened properly to his barks. Could he be right? Could Alice's new house really be just around the corner?

The dog's owner caught up with him and clipped his lead back on, just in time to be yanked off his feet, as his dog charged off again.

"Rufus, what on earth has got into you?" protested the mystified owner, digging in his heels and straining backwards. He was far too busy trying to brake to notice the bedraggled little kitten, trailing along behind them, and the crow, flapping down to half-hop and half-fly along the ground beside her.

The dog dragged his owner a whole block, and then stopped abruptly in front of a lamppost, where the poster of Rosie flapped.

And then he set up a volley of barking, as his horrified owner tried desperately to shush him.

The front door opened. And abruptly, the dog stopped barking.

Alice stood on the doorstep.

"I'm really, terribly sorry," stammered the man, "My dog...well...he seems to know this house..."

"Don't worry," said Alice's mother, coming up behind her. And just as her mother turned away, shutting the door, Alice heard a familiar sound.

It was a weak *meeiou! meeiou!*

"Wait Mum, what's that?" she said, ducking down under her mother's arm. She ran down the front steps and looked around.

A bedraggled scrap of kitten sat on the pavement, mewing up at Alice.

"Oh, you poor little thing," said Alice.

"You're lost..."

She knelt down. The little kitten looked just like Rosie, but she was thinner and darker.

It's me! miaowed Rosie, *I'm still me! I'm just all wet and dirty!*

"Rosie?" said Alice, picking her up.

"Mum!" she called, her voice husky. "Come quickly! It's Rosie!"

And then Rosie gave another squeaky

miaow, and Alice really did believe it. Her lost kitten had somehow managed to find her way home!

"Mum, it's Rosie!"

"Really?" said Alice's mother, coming up behind them. "But it can't be her, surely?"

Miaow-miaow-miaow! said Rosie proudly, launching into a deafening purr. *I'm hungry… And where's Grandma?*

"You are the cleverest, bravest wild-kitten in the whole world," said Alice, blinking away her tears, and she took her kitten inside to give her an enormous bowl of fishy snacks, and to call her Grandma.

Watching from the fence, Charlie the crow gave a satisfied croak, and turned his beak to sort through his tail feathers. Then he shook out his wings and flew off to update Gypsy.

If you liked this book then don't miss...

In this heart-warming Christmas story we meet Milo, the cutest Labrador puppy in town!